The Night Before
A Canadian Christmas

Cover Design by Jennifer Harrington

Printed in Canada by Friesens

Library and Archives Canada Cataloguing in Publication

Townsin, Troy, 1975-
The Night Before A Canadian Christmas / by Troy Townsin; illustrated by Jennifer Harrington.
Special Thanks to Mike Arnott for his help with character development.

ISBN 978-0-9868892-2-6

1. Christmas stories, Canadian (English).
2. Canada--Juvenile fiction.
I. Harrington, Jennifer, 1973- II. Title.

PS8639.O998N54 2011   jC813'.6   C2011-905388-8

The Night Before
A Canadian Christmas

By Troy Townsin
Illustrated by Jennifer Harrington

www.amooseinamapletree.com

'Twas the night before Christmas,
and all around the house,
not a creature was stirring,
except for a moose.
When the lights had been hung
in the front yard with care,
no one had expected
a moose to pass there.

Mom, in her housecoat, turned on the TV and on came the hockey game on CBC.

From the snow-shovelled driveway
there came such a clatter,
I leapt from the chesterfield
to see what was the matter.
The moose had been spooked
by something in the sky,
some thing in the distance,
too far for my eyes...

As the northern lights sparkled
over fresh fallen snow,
the moose fled the scene
with my skidoo in tow!

Mom pointed and screamed,
but I didn't believe her.
She said, "Look, it's a sled
pulled by eight flying beaver!"
With a bearded old driver
in a big bright red tuque,
either it was Santa,
or I was a kook.

Faster than an oncoming **CPR** train,
they hurtled towards us
as he called them by name:
"Now, Gretzky! Now, Trudeau!
Now, Shania and Loonie!
On, Bob! And on, Doug!
On, Suzuki and Toonie!"

"Forget the chimney," cried Santa Claus
with a roar, "there's smoke so we'd
better just use the back door!"
For all over Canada, on this cold
winter's night, for warmth
everyone had their fires alight.

So with a full load of toys
to the back deck they flew,
where they landed beside
the old barbeque.
Then Santa came in while
the beavers took rest -

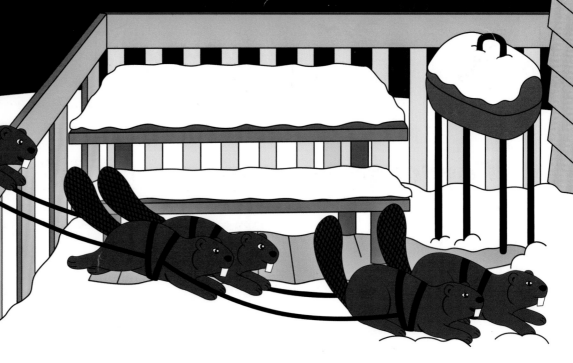

it was then that I noticed
how Santa was dressed...

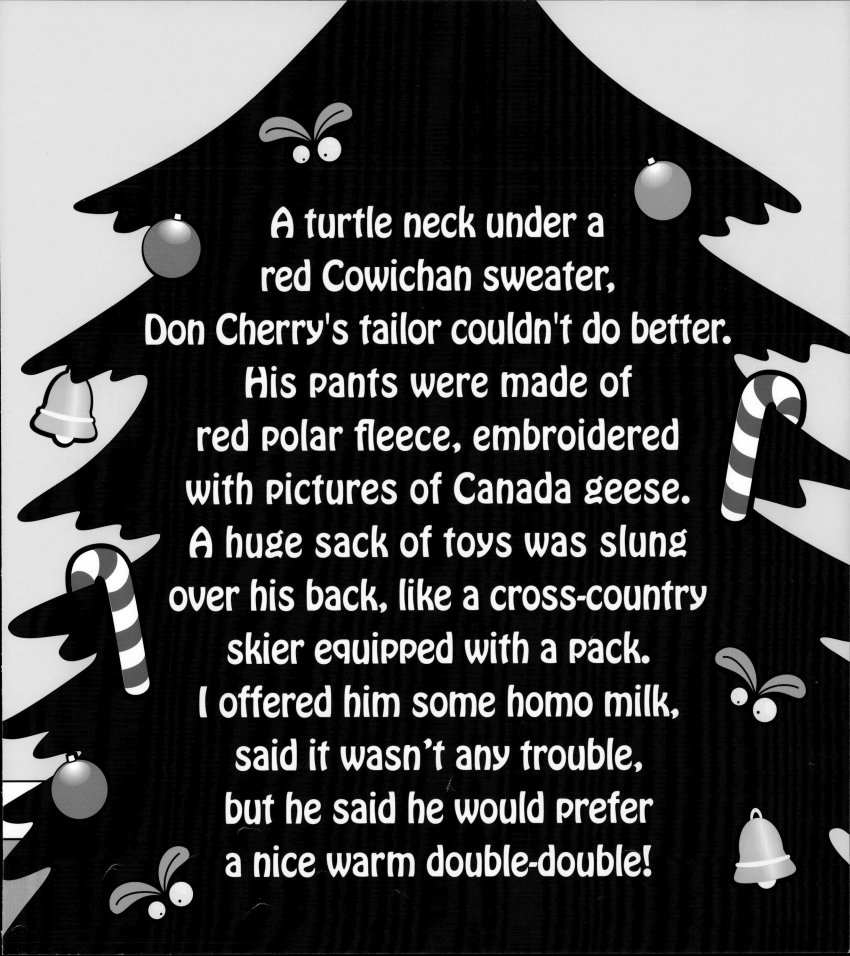

A turtle neck under a
red Cowichan sweater,
Don Cherry's tailor couldn't do better.
His pants were made of
red polar fleece, embroidered
with pictures of Canada geese.
A huge sack of toys was slung
over his back, like a cross-country
skier equipped with a pack.
I offered him some homo milk,
said it wasn't any trouble,
but he said he would prefer
a nice warm double-double!

From his head to his boots
he was covered in snow,
he had frozen eyelashes,
it was 30 below!
He had fluffy white eyebrows
with bright eyes underneath,
and his beard had the appearance
of a big white maple leaf.
He had a lumberjack's physique,
except for his potbelly,
that shook when he laughed
like a salad made of jelly.

He put gifts in all the stockings and around the Christmas tree - there were wonders there for everyone, everyone but ME!

There were snowshoes for the kids
that they would use on Christmas day
and to Mom he gave a blanket
which came from Hudson's Bay.
Then he handed me a present
and I knew I was in luck -
a brand new set of tire chains
for my pickup truck!

He touched his finger to his nose and
just stepped out into the night,

where his beaver team were on
the deck having a snowball fight.

He whistled and they all took
their places at the sled,
and took off through the sky
in a streaking blur of red.

And this is what he shouted
as they up and flew away:

"Merry Christmas Canada
and to all a good night - eh!"

This book is dedicated to the people of Canada and to all those who visit this wonderful country.

About the Author

Troy Townsin is a proud new Canadian!

Born in Melbourne, Australia, he worked as an actor and playwright before embarking on a round-the-world backpacking extravaganza taking him to several continents. Troy has had many jobs. He has been a Stage Manager in Australia, a Teacher-Trainer in Thailand, a Beverage Manager in the UK, an Information Officer for the United Nations and a Columnist for CBC radio in Canada. Troy has won several awards for his writing, including a prestigious 'Travel Writer of the Year" award with TNT Magazine UK and a 'Gourmand World Cookbook Award'.

Troy fell in love with a Canadian girl, married her and then fell in love with Canada, his new home.

About the Illustrator

Jennifer Harrington is an illustrator and graphic designer who grew up in Vancouver, British Columbia. A trained anthropologist, she decided to follow her childhood passion for the visual arts.

She now lives in Toronto, Ontario, where she runs JSH Graphics, a graphic design company that specializes in corporate branding. Jennifer has illustrated numerous ad campaigns and worked as an art director on magazines in Vancouver, Toronto and London, England.

Others books by Troy and Jennifer:

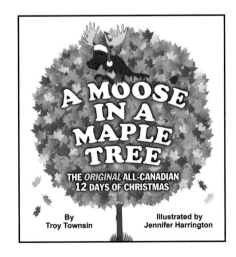

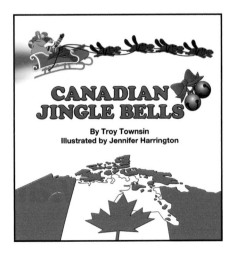